The Rabbit

Illustrations: Marcelle Geneste
Text: Nadine Saunier

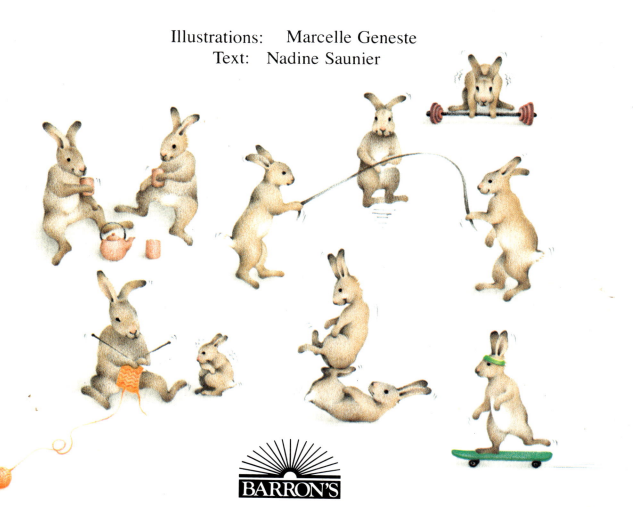

BARRON'S

New York • London • Toronto • Sydney

Neither rain nor
bothers the frisky rabbits.
But the wind makes them run away. With

their   pressed flat against their backs,

they   into their burrows.
They live there in colonies,
which are also called *warrens*.

Some of the words in this book are replaced by pictures.
These pictures reappear and are identified at the end of the book.

When rabbits dig their holes,
nothing is more adorable
than all those little animals with their

 in the air.

Their front paws scratch at the earth, their back

 kick the dirt behind them.

Small mounds indicate
the entrances to these tunnels,
which sometimes are as long as 125 feet.

Rabbits have good appetites.
They devour dandelions,  and alfalfa.
On summer nights, these little rascals

nibble and lettuce in the garden.

They also damage forests
by gnawing away at the bark of trees.
Rabbits don't drink water.
Instead, they lick the dew
that the night sprinkles on the   .

The rabbit is a fearful animal.
His long ears move constantly.
On the prairie each rabbit does his best

 to   his own group.

At the first sign of danger, a rabbit
to warn the others.
Foxes, weasels, and other animals are all to be
feared — and so are people and their guns.

It is mating season.
The male does all kinds of funny 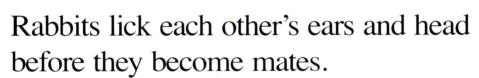 .

Rabbits lick each other's ears and head
before they become mates.
A month later, the mother rabbit

will nurse her  .

Before having her  ,
the mother rabbit digs a new burrow
with a big area in the back for a nursery.
With straw, dry grass, and hay,

she builds a soft  .   From

one to  little ones,
each weighing scarcely two ounces,
will be born there, safe from the male,
who might harm them.

The newborns are blind and deaf.

At and dusk,
the mother nurses her babies.
After each visit,
she closes the entrance to the nursery.
The badger, the ermine, or the ferret would

gladly enter and eat the .
After three weeks, the mother and her babies
join the other rabbits' big warren.

Rabbits have babies six times each year.
Before long, young ones begin doing the same.
Rabbits can become so numerous,
they sometimes overwhelm
a huge area, as they
have done in the land
of kangaroos:

All over the world,
one finds different kinds of rabbits.
Those from Japan, India, and Mexico
are the rarest.

The  rabbits
weigh
between
fifteen
and
twenty

pounds, and are white or silver.
The chinchillas have the finest fur.
But the nicest of all are the dwarf rabbits.
Children like them best.

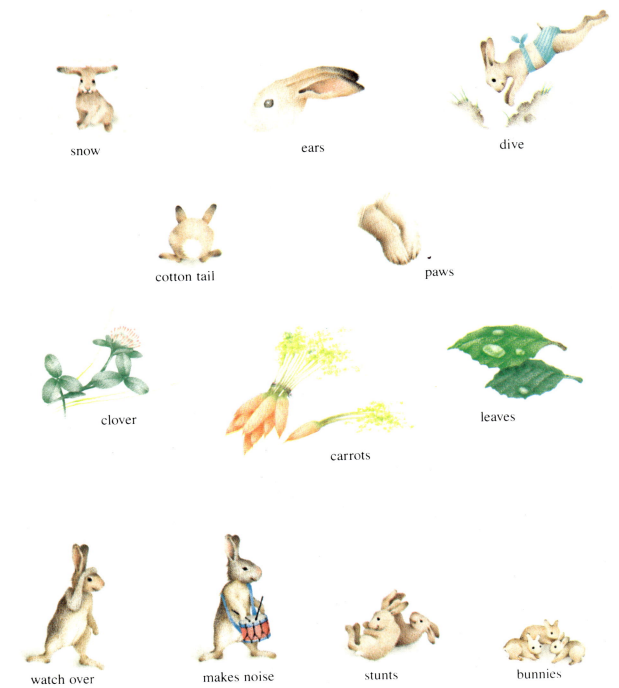

snow

ears

dive

cotton tail

paws

clover

carrots

leaves

watch over

makes noise

stunts

bunnies